柔　　然
~uanruan

~元386）呼和浩特
　　　建國號魏
D. 386) Wei nation
~ablished at Hohhot

~元398）遷都大同稱皇帝
D. 398) Wei leader
~wned himself Emperor,
~ital moved to Datung

二　　魏
~rthern　Wei

~元493）遷都洛陽
D. 493) Capital
~ved to Luoyang

鮮卑原居地
Original location of Xianbei people
（約公元200）
(c. A.D. 200)

燕　山
Yanshan

黃　河
Yellow　River

長　江
Yangtze　River

南　　　朝
Southern　Dynasty

北魏文化
ND ITS CULTURE

水經注

扉頁上的北魏藝術作品插圖說明

Artifacts from the Northern Wei Dynasty Illustrated on Endleaves

左邊的插圖　　　（由上而下）
LEFT (FROM TOP TO BOTTOM)

1. 北魏陶俑三尊：午女、文官、武將

   Baked clay figurines from a tomb: dancing girl, scholar-official, general.

2. 屏風漆畫：列女古賢圖之局部

   Detail from a painted lacquer screen: illustrated stories of virtuous men and women.

3. 書法：魏碑鄭長猷造像

   Calligraphy in the Tablet style: rubbing from Wei stone stele announcing the dedication of a sculpted Buddha to a gentleman's son.

4. 瓷器：青瓷蓮花尊 石刻神怪（背景）

   Porcelain: celadon (gray-green) jar with lotus pattern. Background: stone carving of mythical creatures.

5. 雕塑：鮮卑族童男 甘肅省麥積山石窟

   Sculpture: Xianbei boy, from Maijishan Grottos in Gansu province.

右邊的插圖　　　（由上而下）
RIGHT (FROM TOP TO BOTTOM)

1. 雕塑：大佛　山西省雲崗石窟

   Sculpture: large Buddha from Yungang Grottos in Shanxi province.

2. 壁畫：狩獵圖　甘肅省敦煌莫高窟

   Wall painting: hunting scene from Mogao Grotto in Dunhuang, Gansu.

3. 地理學著作：水經注 北魏酈道元著

   A forty-volume geography text, *The Water Chronicles,* by Li Daoyuan.

4. 錢幣：太和五銖　　北魏孝文帝時造
   （背景）　　　北魏織錦　樹紋

   Foreground: a coin worth 5 *ju* minted in the reign of Emperor Xiaowen.

   Background: woven silk brocade fabric with stylized tree pattern.

5. 雕塑：鮮卑族童女 甘肅省麥積山石窟

   Sculpture: Xianbei girl, from Maijishan Grottos in Gansu province.

The Ballad of
MULAN

To Jake
From Moéinte + Pappy
With much love
xxx
Oct. 2005

— For everyone with an
interest in ancient Chinese
culture and literature. S.N.Z.

Copyright © 1998 by Song Nan Zhang

Published in the United States of America by
Pan Asian Publications (USA) Inc.
29564 Union City Blvd., Union City, CA 94587

Tel. (510) 475-1185   Fax (510) 475-1489

ISBN 1-57227-054-3
Library of Congress Catalog Card Number: 97-80575

Editorial and production assistance: William Mersereau, Art & Publishing Consultants

Printed in Hong Kong

The Ballad of
MULAN

Retold and illustrated by
Song Nan Zhang

Pan Asian Publications

唧唧復唧唧木蘭當戶織 不聞機杼聲惟聞女嘆息

木蘭辭　北朝樂府

Long ago, in a village in northern China, there lived a girl named Mulan. One day, she sat at her loom weaving cloth. *Click-clack! Click-clack!* went the loom.

女亦無所思　女亦無所憶
問女何所思　問女何所憶

木蘭辞　北朝樂府

Suddenly, the sound of weaving changed to sorrowful sighs.
"What troubles you?" her mother asked.
"Nothing, Mother," Mulan softly replied.

昨晚見軍帖可汗大點兵

木蘭辭　北朝樂府

Her mother asked her again and again, until Mulan finally said,
"There is news of war."

木蘭辭　北朝樂府

軍書十二卷卷卷有爺名

"Invaders are attacking. The Emperor is calling for troops.
Last night, I saw the draft poster and twelve scrolls of names
in the market. Father's name is on every one."

阿爺無大兒木蘭無長兄

"But Father is old and frail," Mulan sighed. "How can he fight? He has no grown son and I have no elder brother."

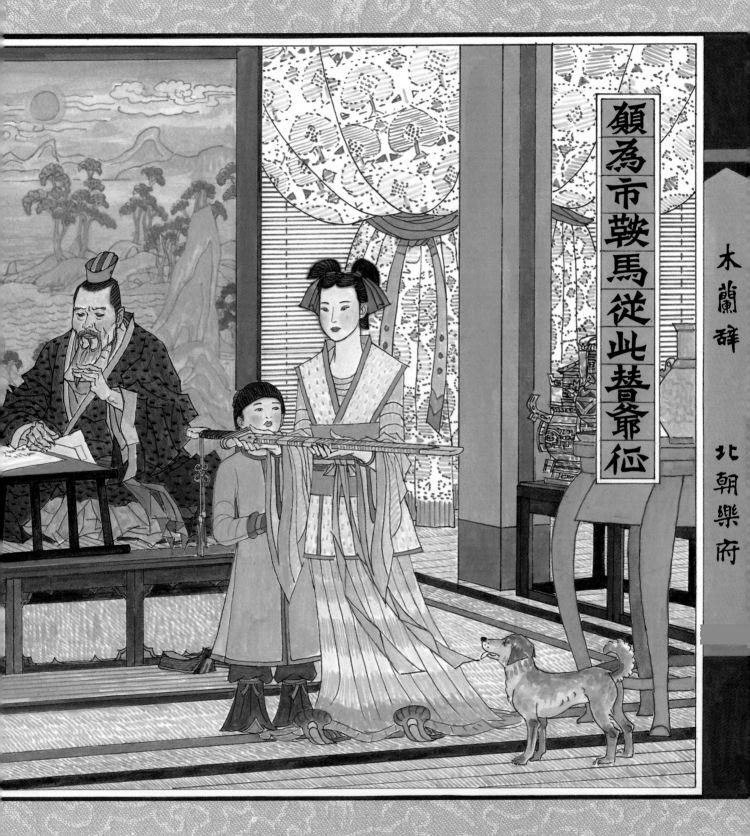

願為市鞍馬從此替爺征

木蘭辭　北朝樂府

"I will go to the markets. I shall buy a saddle and a horse.
I must fight in Father's place."

東市買駿馬西市買鞍韉

木蘭辭　北朝樂府

From the eastern market Mulan bought a horse,
and from the western market, a saddle.
From the northern market she bought a bridle,
and from the southern market, a whip.

南市買轡頭北市買長鞭

木蘭辭 北朝樂府

At dawn Mulan dressed in her armor and bid a sad
farewell to her father, mother, sister, and brother.
Then she mounted her horse and rode off with the soldiers.

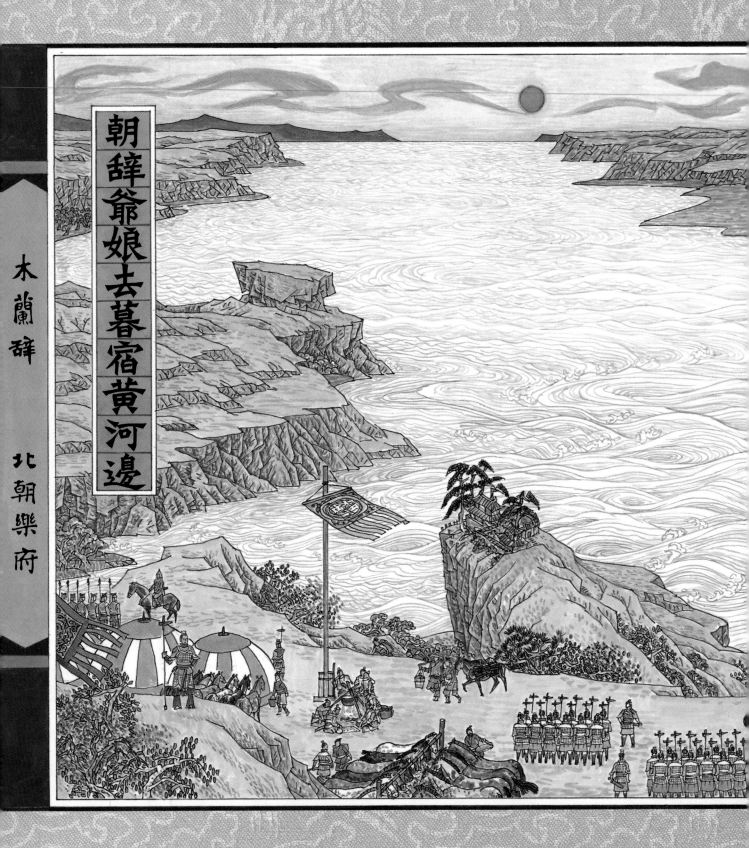

朝辭爺娘去暮宿黃河邊

木蘭辭　北朝樂府

By nightfall she was camped by the bank of the Yellow River.
She thought she heard her mother calling her name.

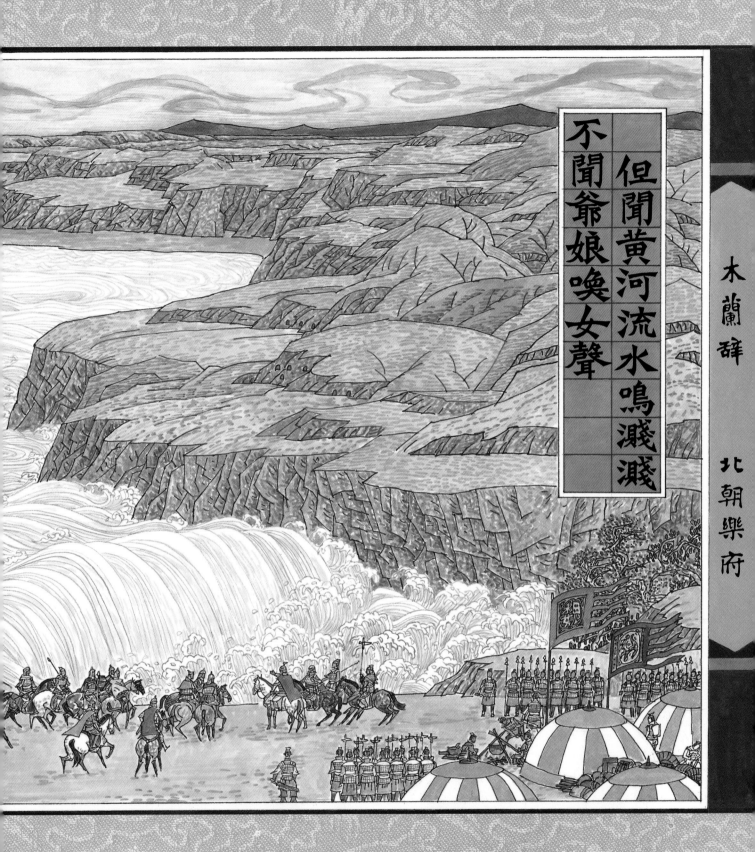

但聞黃河流水鳴濺濺
不聞爺娘喚女聲

木蘭辭　北朝樂府

But it was only the sound of the river crying.

At sunrise Mulan took leave of the Yellow River.
At dusk she reached the peak of Black Mountain.

但聞燕山胡騎聲啾啾
不聞爺娘喚女聲

木蘭辭　北朝樂府

In the darkness she longed to hear her father's voice
but heard only the neighing of enemy horses far away.

萬里赴戎機關山度若飛

木蘭辭　北朝樂府

Mulan rode ten thousand miles to fight a hundred battles.
She crossed peaks and passes like a bird in flight.

朔氣傳金柝寒光照鐵衣

木蘭辭　北朝樂府

Nights at the camp were harsh and cold,
but Mulan endured every hardship.
Knowing her father was safe warmed her heart.

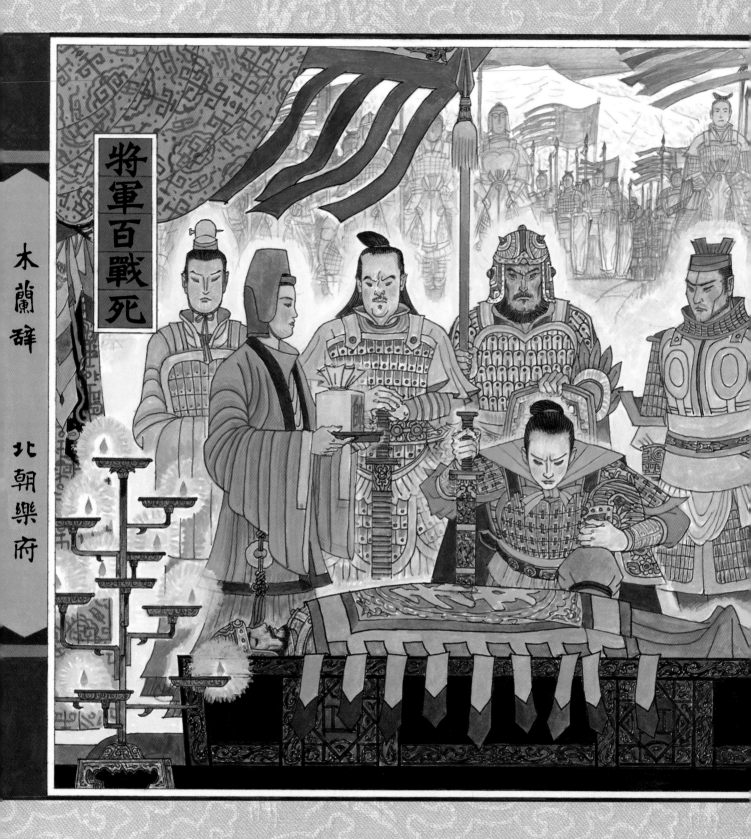

将军百战死

木蘭辭 北朝樂府

The war dragged on. Fierce battles ravaged the land.
One after another, noble generals lost their lives.

壮士十年歸

木蘭辭　北朝樂府

Mulan's skill and courage won her respect and rank.
After ten years, she returned as a great general,
triumphant and victorious!

歸來見天子天子坐明堂

The Emperor summoned Mulan to the High Palace.
He praised her for her bravery and leadership in battle.

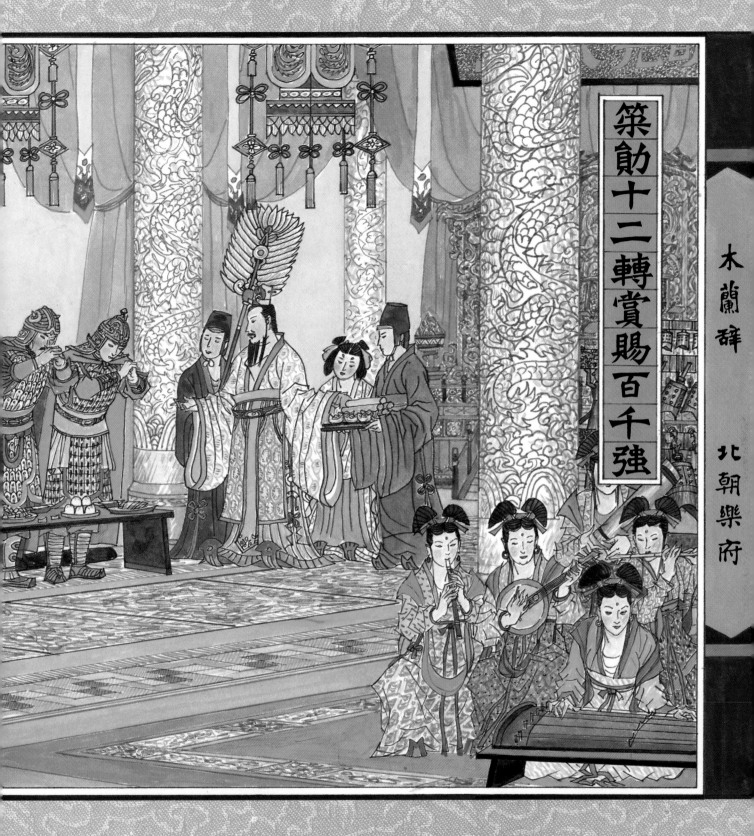

策勳十二轉賞賜百千強

木蘭辭　北朝樂府

The Court would bestow many great titles upon her.
Mulan would be showered with gifts of gold.

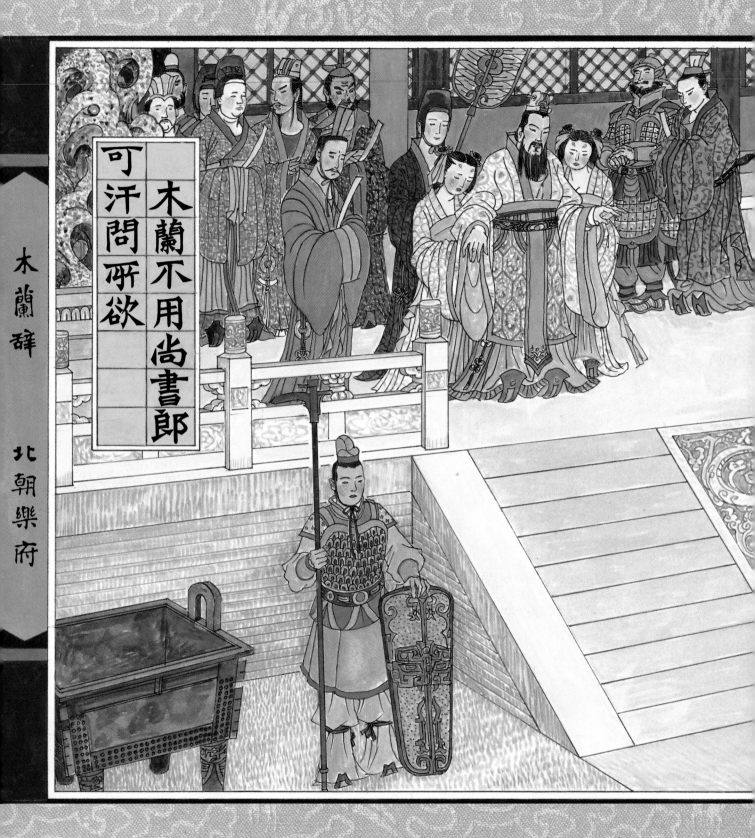

木蘭辭　北朝樂府

可汗問所欲　木蘭不用尚書郎

"Worthy General, you may have your heart's desire,"
the Emperor said.
"I have no need for honors or gold," Mulan replied.

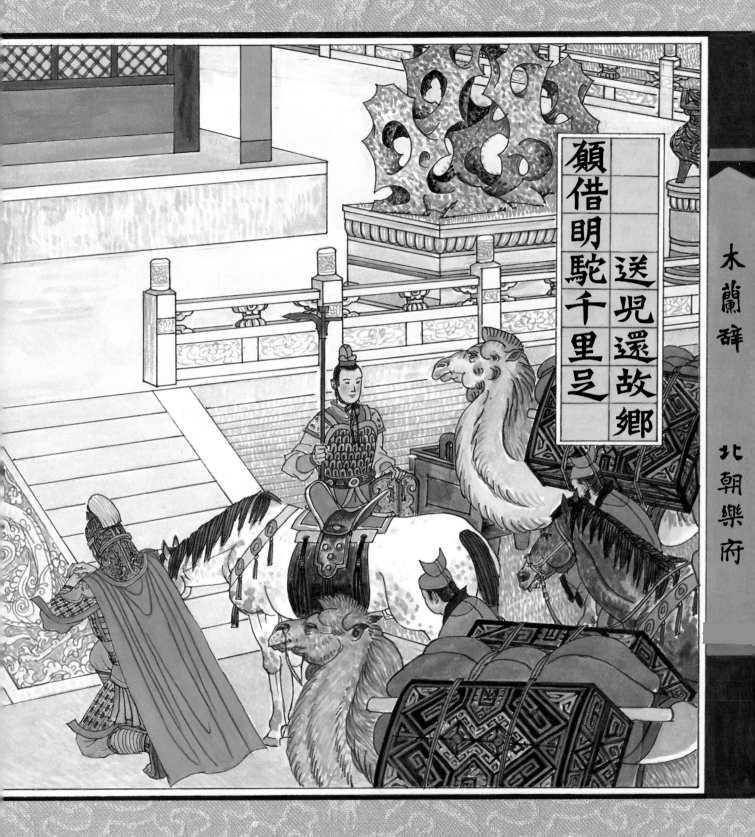

願借明駝千里足　送兒還故鄉

木蘭辭　北朝樂府

"All I ask for is a swift camel to take me back home."
The Emperor sent a troop to escort Mulan on her trip.

木蘭辭　北朝樂府

阿姊聞妹來當戶理紅妝
爺娘聞女來出廓相扶將

In town, the news of Mulan's return created great
excitement. Holding each other, her proud parents
walked to the village gate to welcome her.

小弟聞姊來　磨刀霍霍向豬羊

木蘭辭　北朝樂府

Waiting at home, Mulan's sister beautified herself.
Her brother sharpened his knife to prepare a pig and sheep
for the feast in Mulan's honor.

脱我戰時袍著我舊時裳
開我東閣門坐我西閣床

木蘭辭　北朝樂府

Home at last! Mulan threw open her bedroom door
and smiled. She removed her armor and changed
into one of her favorite dresses.

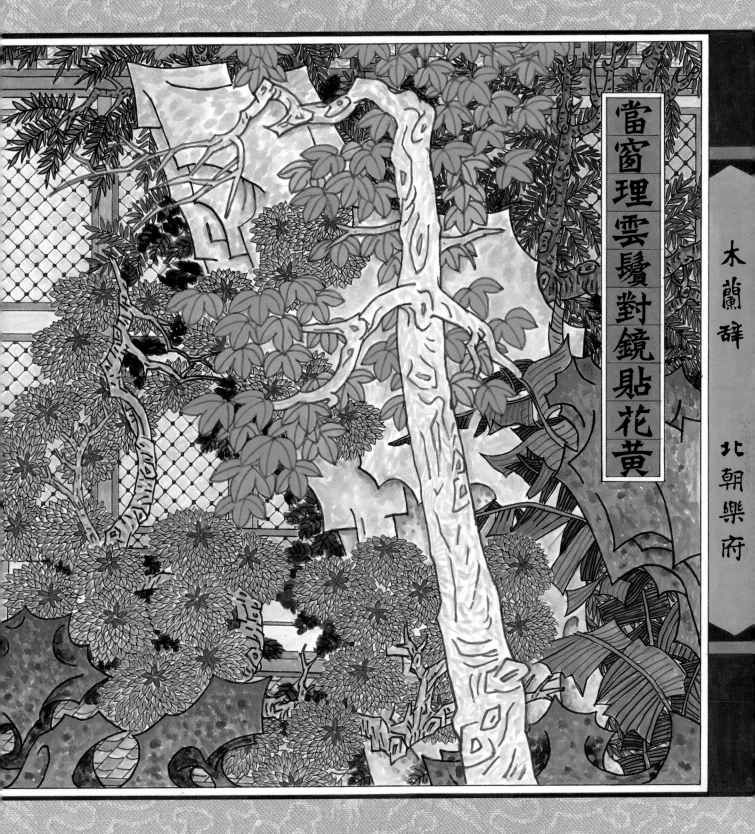

當窗理雲鬢對鏡貼花黄

木蘭辭

北朝樂府

She brushed out her shiny black hair and pasted
a yellow flower on her face. She looked into the mirror
and smiled again, happy to be home.

木蘭辭　北朝樂府

出門看伙伴伙伴皆惊惶

What a surprise it was when Mulan appeared at the door!
Her comrades were astonished and amazed.
"How is this possible?" they asked.

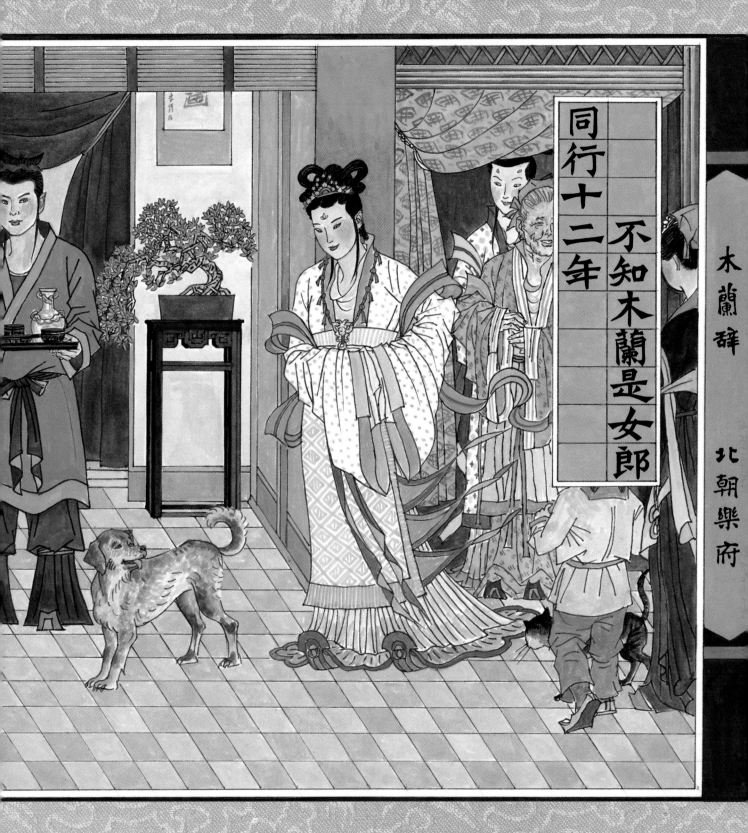

木蘭辭　北朝樂府

同行十二年　不知木蘭是女郎

"How could we have fought side by side
with you for ten years and not have known
you were a woman!"

雄兔腳撲朔雌兔眼迷離

木蘭辭　北朝樂府

Mulan replied, "They say the male rabbit likes to hop
and leap, while the female rabbit prefers to sit still.
But in times of danger, when the two rabbits scurry by,
who can tell male from female?"

雙兔傍地走安能辨我是雄雌

木蘭辭　北朝樂府

Mulan's glory spread through the land. And to this day,
we sing of this brave woman who loved her family
and served her country, asking for nothing in return.

HISTORICAL NOTES ON MULAN

The end of the highly civilized Han dynasty in AD 220 was followed by three centuries of bitter civil war, invasion, and unstable governments which threatened the very future of Chinese civilization. In the fourth and fifth centuries, northern China was repeatedly attacked from foreign tribes, and experienced almost constant warfare, anarchy and devastation before the Tuoba clan, of the foreign Xianbei culture, established a unified regime in 386 which became the Northern Wei dynasty (386–534). The Xianbei were originally tough nomads and excellent horsemen who came from what is now the north of Inner Mongolia.

To maintain their control over the Han Chinese majority, some 20 million people, the Northern Wei rulers adopted more and more Chinese customs and institutions. They eventually took Han surnames, adopted Chinese dress and language in court, and intermarried with the Han nobility. They also played a major role in the spread of the new Buddhist religion. Despite their assimilation into Chinese culture, or 'sinicization,' strong tribal customs endured. They emphasized military rule over civilized and bureaucratized government. The foreign control of government, however, actually kept the courts open to central and western Asiatic cultural influences, making it a very multicultural period in Chinese history. Before it was sacked in 524, the new capital in Luoyang boasted half a million inhabitants with many large, magnificent palaces and mansions, and over a thousand Buddhist monasteries.

It was during the Northern Wei period that the ballad of Mulan was composed as a popular song before being officially sanctioned by the court. Whether Mulan's story was based on an actual case of a victorious female general is unknown, but her independant spirit and martial skills clearly suggest her origin in the nomadic–warrior Xianbei culture, rather than Han culture, where women's roles were more rigidly defined.

The earliest known written version of the poem is found in an anthology of dynastic folk poetry (*yuefu*) compiled during the Song dynasty (960–1279). In this Song version (which is incorporated into the illustrations of this book), the heroine is known simply as Mulan, which means 'magnolia.' The poem was later made into a poetic musical drama (*zaju*) by a great Ming dynasty scholar, and then expanded into a novel in the late Ming (1368-1644). These and other later versions often give a family name to Mulan, such as Hua (flower). Passed down from generation to generation, Mulan remains a widely known folk heroine throughout China where school children still learn the poem by heart. As a symbol, Mulan continues to inspire Chinese girls and women with the belief that women—if given the opportunity—are capable of accomplishing all the same feats as men. Her heroism, her loyalty to country and devotion to family, continue to provide the basis for countless Chinese poems, essays, operas, paintings, and, more recently, animated films and comic books.

木兰辞*

唧唧复唧唧，木兰当户织。不闻机杼声，唯闻女叹息。
问女何所思，问女何所忆？"女亦无所思，女亦无所忆。
昨夜见军帖，可汗大点兵，军书十二卷，卷卷有爷名。
阿爷无大儿，木兰无长兄，愿为市鞍马，从此替爷征。"

东市买骏马，西市买鞍鞯，南市买辔头，北市买长鞭。
旦辞爷娘去，暮宿黄河边。不闻爷娘唤女声，但闻黄河流水鸣溅溅。
旦辞黄河去，暮至黑山头。不闻爷娘唤女声，但闻燕山胡骑鸣啾啾。

万里赴戎机，关山度若飞。朔气传金柝，寒光照铁衣。
将军百战死，壮士十年归。归来见天子，天子坐明堂。
策勋十二转，赏赐百千强。可汗问所欲，"木兰不用尚书郎，
愿借明驼千里足，送儿还故乡。"

爷娘闻女来，出郭相扶将。阿姊闻妹来，当户理红妆。
小弟闻姊来，磨刀霍霍向猪羊。开我东阁门，坐我西阁床。
脱我战时袍，著我旧时裳。当窗理云鬓，对镜贴花黄。
出门看伙伴，伙伴皆惊惶。同行十二年，不知木兰是女郎。

"雄兔脚扑朔，雌兔眼迷离；
双兔傍地走，安能辨我是雄雌？"

The Ballad of Mulan in simplified Chinese characters

鮮卑族興起年代及路線
Xianbei nation's rise and migration

木蘭從軍出征路線
Mulan's journey to the frontline

長城
The Great Wall

今日中國邊界
Chinese borders today

北魏（A.D. 386-53
THE NORTHERN W